EBONY ORMOND-HAM

Three Times A Lady: The Woman. Her Business. Her God.
Copyright © 2018 Ebony Ormond-Ham

All rights reserved. No part of this publication
may be reproduced, distributed, or transmitted in any form
or by any means, including photocopying, recording, or other
electronic or mechanical methods, without the prior
written permission of the Author.

Panagiotis Lampridis Book Cover Designs
Cover Design

DHBonner Virtual Solutions LLC
Interior Format & Layout | Author Coaching
www.dhbonner.net

Scripture unless otherwise indicated taken from the Holy Bible,
NEW INTERNATIONAL VERSION ®, NIV ® Copyright © 1973,
1978, 1984, 2011 by Biblica, Inc. ® Used by permission. All rights
reserved worldwide.

ISBN: 978-0-692-11926-6

Printed in the United States of America

Dedication

In every stage of my life, God threw me a lifeline. So, this book is dedicated to the individuals that I credit my growth to. Thank you to my Grandmother, Mary Glenn Jones. It's hard to think of you and not shed tears.

You've taught me lessons even when you weren't physically in my presence. I don't know if I would have chosen life on many occasions without your consistent love and support. I feel your hand in my back; pushing me into dimensions that I really want to accomplish just to show you that your work, love, and unconditional support of me is not in vain.

You are my lifeline.

To my Mom, Lalonnie Rankin: Having a best friend in a Mother has been one of the greatest experiences. You have given me everything that you had in you to give, and I want you to know that "IT WAS ENOUGH".

Thank you for loving me unconditionally and supporting me throughout these 36 years of life.

I am… because of you.

To my Dad, Dalton Lee Jones: Growing up, many of my friends had the unfortunate testimony of their father not being present. I am so grateful to God that I wasn't able to share in that pain with them. I don't ever remember you not being there.

My entrepreneurial spirit is often accredited to you. Thank you for being one of the most amazing men that I've ever known.

My first love.

Lastly, to my grandmother Joyce Ormond: Grandmothers are some of the rarest and most valuable gifts that a child is afforded. You were, and have continued to be, the rock of the Ormond family.

Even through disappointments, you remain the glue to many broken pieces. Thank you for always being our protector. Thank you for being present. Thank you for every pair of sneakers you bought to encourage my love of basketball.

You are, and will forever be, my "Diva J".

Table of Contents

Foreword...i
A Letter of Love for Ebony................................... vi
Lifelines 4
The Woman 24
    I've Got Confidence 30
    The Miscarriages 35
    Promise Reminder (The Miracle) 39
Her Business 44
    Women and Business 54
    Setting Business Goals 59
    Financial Planning 68
    Millionaire Mindset 73
Her God 79
    In The Beginning 79
    The Present 86
Feminine Financial Quotes 93
Spiritual Financial Quotes 98

Cast not away therefore your confidence, which hath great recompence of reward. For ye have need of patience, that, after ye have done the will of God, ye might receive the promise.

~ Hebrews 10:35-36 (KJV)

Foreword

It is a well-documented fact that a child born into adversity is at an increased risk of experiencing many negative outcomes in their life. It has also been said that a child's living conditions, exposure to aggression, substance abuse, violence, and physical abuse will dampen their views on life, love, and success.

However, although this *"Three Times a Lady"* Author was a resident of those adverse conditions, she is not a product of her circumstance. Having had her own share of 'ups and downs', Ebony has made the choice, over and over... and over again, to keep breathing; for herself, for her family, and for others. To never forget the lessons learned from her grandmother, her mother, her father, and the many others who appeared in her life, just when she needed them the most. And, to be a living example for others of what God can do when you entrust Him with your life… the past, the present, and the future.

In this book, *"Three Times A Lady: The Woman. Her Business. Her God."* you will read about the childhood memories of a female entrepreneur. Memories of childhood molestation, memories of senseless violence in her community, and memories of the people God always had assigned to support her. 'Rescuers' who came in many different forms; such as, school teachers, pastors, principals, neighbors, drug dealers, and prostitutes.

Lifelines that have not been forgotten.

Ebony and I first met during a wedding at the Maury Chapel Free Will Baptist Church in Maury, North Carolina. I was attending the wedding of my god-brother; which is her cousin. After being introduced to her by her cousins, we were supposed to go out on a date, but the choir she was involved in at the time was preparing for their choir anniversary, *and she stood me up.*

Truth be told, by now, some of the exact facts have been forgotten, and Ebony teases me that I have begun making some parts up. *Nevertheless,* no matter how it all came about, suffice it to say, that once we were able to spend time together, I am glad that this was one chance meeting I did not miss.

We hit it off pretty well, and I quickly learned that there were so many facets to Ebony.

She is athletic, lady-like, and a beautiful soul.

An Entrepreneur, a Strategist, and a Fighter.

A woman who operates in a spirit of excellence; with an internal purpose so instinctive, that nothing can extinguish it. Not because she doesn't have struggles or have to push her way through; nor because she is immune to pain or beyond the devastation of loss and grief. But, simply because she has made the decision to never give up… that even if life pushes her and demands that she bend, she refuses to break!

Much like anyone else, I have watched Ebony encounter critical points in her life where she had to face defining moments; forced to simply make a choice. And, each time, I have been witness to her choosing to demonstrate that her life's journey couldn't simply be contained by the broken pieces of this world.

Instead, she decided to step out of the shadows and the poverty-stricken wastelands of her environment and create a life worth living; a life that has changed my perspective of in general!

I'm sure that if you were to ask around, her contributions to others have been far beyond selfless. Still more importantly, she has shown me how to build a legacy and envision something greater for myself than I knew this world had to offer.

"Three Times A Lady: The Woman. Her Business. Her God" is a glimpse into the pain of Ebony's life. However, it is not a story of defeat. It is a story of an overcomer... and a celebration of those who have come alongside her, to breathe life into her... so that she can now breathe life into so many others.

I am grateful to be one of those.

Andre Ham
CEO; Clark Atlanta Healthcare Services, LLC
Atlanta, GA

A Letter of Love for Ebony

Hi Ebony,

I really don't know how to write this letter to express how I really feel about you. I have so much that I want to say to you and cannot express it all; it is too much for me to write, and each line would only be filled with words from my repertoire that I continually add to over time. (haha)

You were born January the 29th, 1982, at 12:45. And, I was right there. I knew then, that you had a uniqueness about you that would surpass anything that some people could even imagine.

And then, when we brought you out of the hospital, you had already become *my* baby, as opposed to Lalonnie's, to the point that I had become like jealous of her; knowing that *she* was your mom. Still, I wanted to make sure that you received everything you needed, so that you could grow up and become the woman that you are today.

Even though we cannot measure Love, I know that the Love Dre has for you is great. He is an asset to you Ebony, and I believe that God has joined you and Dre together for something special; especially for Cameron.

That's Mawmaw's baby.

There is so much, I cannot tell it all! I have never asked anything of you that you haven't come through for me... You haven't been perfect. No one is. But, you are as much my daughter as my four boys are my sons. I am proud of what you've accomplished.

Ebony, what I am trying to say is that you have been the kind of granddaughter that any grandmother would be proud of. You have shown so much care for me. So much so, until I really don't know how to receive it all. I know I've said this a thousand times, but thank you so much for having my kitchen built. Every time I walk in there, tears run down my face. What a beautiful gift from my granddaughter. I have been blessed by all of my children.

You have made my life complete... full of joy and happiness. So, I am closing this letter with much love, and *thank you!* Thank you for being all that you can be through your business, through your ministry, through your teaching... through your life. For doing all you can do and leaving the rest in the hands of the Lord.

I love you!

~Grandma

Introduction

It's a wonder that my knees aren't scarred. It's a wonder that the heart isn't deteriorated, because as much as my Grandmother kept me kneeling to pray, those prayers weren't enough to keep the very people ordained by God to love me, from scarring my soul.

So, we'll get familiar early with the devastations of molestation and the visuals of the cream semen that tormented my mind for years.

Right now, in this instance, is the only time that you'll know of that pain. And don't bother to ask because you'll never know my pain by NAME. I'm not here to sing the dis-cord of my heart's song. I'm here to build you up with my truths, my victories; the transparencies of me.

Let me share with you my soul.

My SOUL, the only part of me that can't lie.

> **"Transparency is the first dimension of success."**
>
> ~Ebony Ormond Ham

Transparency gives us the opportunity to separate ourselves from what the enemy can hold over our heads as a wager for life's sins, and when we expose our-self, we free ourselves from within.

Summer breaks, or holidays in general, especially for children, are supposed to be joyous and prissy-filled teachable moments that should prepare them for the maturities of life.

And, although we are taught that the stresses of life are to make us stronger, I'm wondering why molesters aren't brought up to speed as to how entering a young girl, has the ability to destroy her chances of carrying out her God-given assignment to be a nurturer; a Mother.

The many miscarriages that you'll later learn more of… yes, my doctor informed me was a direct result of my cervix being funneled. That trauma has caused me so much pain and confusion.

I've detailed that only to say that this is the only time that I can remember being angry about it.

And, to this day, I don't know why I don't hate the individual. As devastating as the instances were and have been for me, even now, I don't hate him. Yet, here was this person, who had so deeply harmed me, and while I would later lose gifts of great value from my womb, he is still walking around like nothing happened.

Still, his name will remain between me and God, but I needed to free myself; even if, but for this very moment.

I need to heal.

That one situation has caused me to put up a facade that I know has wounded others. It caused me to treat all relationships and friendships as if the hurt would be done before I let you attempt to get close; and boy do I feel sorry for the many leaders who tried to nurture my gifts.

You really didn't stand a chance because my respect for authority at one point was nonexistent.

So, I've lost friendships, relationships, and even struggled to be a wife; yet, it has made me a pretty spiffy entrepreneur, because I was determined that no one else was going to hurt me... or tell me what to do.

Thankfully, God blessed me with individuals who could see me, in spite of the pain; those who had an abundance of compassion to support me in traversing the land mines of devastation in my childhood to the faith-fueled victory of my womanhood.

Thank You, Lord for my Lifelines...

Lifelines

More than three decades of life's lessons originally started with the voice and influence of my grandmother.

The letter you just read from her is the essence of what we've shared; and please understand that this is the very first time that I've read the words she penned to me.
I wanted to wait until this book was published to read them myself. Before this, the very first word I remember learning from her was *"ceiling"*.

Gawmaw, as I call her, taught me that word. However, she didn't just teach me the word; she also shared a lesson about ceilings that has stuck with me throughout the past 36 years of my life. That word has helped me to encourage and provoke many that I've come into contact with to break glass ceilings and dream in a realm that is not foreseen by the natural eye.

She encouraged me to know that anything tangible was obtainable.

And, I believe her.

"You can achieve anything higher than yourself."

Growing up in Durham, NC afforded me a lot of hidden treasures; treasures that weren't really considered to be so, unless like me, you're anointed to see victory in a distorted picture.

This distorted picture made me who I am... A woman of faith. My faith has never failed me, but it was hard to comprehend. It was spooky, it was scary, and at the same time, it was exciting. I was your walking Matilda, Vickie the Robot, and Pippi Longstocking. I was practically in a world of my own where I was princess and heroine.

From a little redhead girl until now, there was this unexplainable gift that I have always had; to force my mind to believe in the very thing which hadn't yet manifested. Faith has always intrigued me, and still to this day, I wonder how does such an amazing God give substance to a thing without form?

It has become my own personal gateway to things not yet seen. The Bible calls it a substance, so isn't it only just a matter of time? Faith has to create!

From the onset, I knew the life that I wanted to live, and more importantly, I understood that *speaking of it* helped it to show up.

> **"I never have any difficulty believing in miracles, since I experienced the miracle of a change in my own heart."**
> ~Augustine

When did I know for sure that I had it... that I had Faith? It was one of the afternoons I was left to care for my little brother Andrae, known to the family as Anjamont. Things were really tight during this period, and there was barely any food in the house. The pots were empty, and so were the shelves and the fridge. I remember him whimpering because he was hungry.

So hungry that he had begun to cry; beginning with his body shuddering as he silently wept, and soon a loud sob as he clutched his stomach.

What could I do to make him stop crying, and well, satisfy his hunger? Feeling helpless at first, but miraculously humorous at the same time, I told him to go into the kitchen and bring me whatever he found to eat.

When he returned, he had the end piece of a loaf of bread and a cup of water. With a little ray of hope in his eyes, he looked at me. Sensing a presence in my room that at the time I couldn't explain, I instructed him to eat the bread and drink the water, but say, *"This is some good..."* whatever it was that he wanted to eat.

Doing as his big sister instructed, he began saying, "This is some good pizza." "This is a good hamburger." etc." It became hilariously funny to us, and I soon joined in with suggestions of my own. *"Yeah, that's some good chicken wings Anjamont. Let me have a bite, please."*

He would munch on that little slice of bread, chewing loudly, as if he was indeed eating chicken wings.

About five minutes later, my Uncle Maurice knocked on the door. When I opened the door, he was holding five pizzas. Apparently, the carrier had not been able to find the house he was supposed to deliver the order to, and my Uncle just happened to come along at that time and bought the pizzas from him.

I was shocked, frozen at the spot, as my brother yelled in excitement; grinning and looking at me as if I had just made his wishes come true. I remember a feeling flowing through my entire body. It was like an electric shock, and something exploded in me. It was unexplainable that today of all days, this would happen.

This was just the beginning of something great in my life, and as the years passed, my faith continued to manifest miracles. Everywhere I turned, there was a lifeline. I didn't go out looking for these lifelines, they just came to me; the door, the windows, all opening to usher me in. I didn't have to ask, it just happened.

"It's not enough to have lived. We should be determined to live for something. May I suggest that it be creating joy for others, sharing what we have for the betterment of person-kind, bringing hope to the lost, and love to the lonely."
~Leo Buscaglia

Now, allow me to introduce you to a few of these amazing people; without them, I would not have made it.

First, I'd like you to meet Mrs. Hazel P. Crump, my 89 year old best friend.

Mrs. Hazel P. Crump

Mrs. Hazel was my next door neighbor, who baked cakes for rich people, and filled jars with quarters to make sure that I always had food to eat or money for college. She never had kids of her own and her husband had died prior to our meeting her in 1989.

She was a widow with the most gorgeous all-white German Shepherd named Shy, who barely came outdoors, and was treated like he was royalty. She would serve him food on glistening plates that had his name written in gold on them. His chain even had a locket with a picture of him and his owner.

She would say, *"I need him to be brought back as soon as possible if he ever manages to leave the house."*

He was more like a cat, full of pride, with his head held up high as he trotted around the house; finally resting on her bed where he spent most of the day.

We lived beside Mrs. Hazel on Broadway St in Durham. I loved going over to her house, and after school, once I had dropped my bag, I would head right over there and sit out on the front porch waiting for her to come outside.

My love for cakes stemmed from her. It was always amazing watching her in the kitchen. "Break the eggs Ebony." "Turn the flour in." "Too much sugar."

She was so creative, and could bake anything that had flour in it. My stomach was a happy recipient of her pastries, as I enjoyed reaching over and snatching a cookie, or placing the butter icing bowl in front of me while I licked it clean.

Her cakes always turned out so beautiful; the kitchen filled with the aroma. I would watch the delivery boy pull up to receive the cake for delivery, which most times she preferred to do, and then listen to her tell me all about the rich people who were paying a fortune for her cakes.

Mrs. Hazel's nickname for me was "Dollbaby."

She would rave about my having big gorgeous eyes; telling me that they were a gift to always see past the present circumstances. She would also tell me funny and non-child appropriate jokes... that I would think about into the night and laugh over. One joke in particular that she shared with my little brothers, and eventually my husband upon meeting him, was to eat a lot of bananas because it puts lead in their pencils.

Lol... real loud. Those were the good old days.

I believe she saw me more as an adult than a child, and she would share with me that I had an old soul, which was also a gift.

Even when we moved away, I still made sure to come back; and a couple of times, I was able to convince my mother to let me spend the night there.

The Sleepovers were always awesome! We would watch old soaps into the night, and she would speak about her childhood, what a wonderful man her husband had been, as well as what the future could bring for me.

When I left for college, and even after I had gotten married, I always called to check on her or make random trips to Durham, because she would tell me that no one was around to take her to the grocery store.

She still lived in her old house, and was very comfortable; although she kept more to herself by then. Times had simply changed and so did the manners of the neighborhood youth that moved in after we left.

Prior to this, Mrs. Hazel was known as the old lady that took care of all of the children in the neighborhood.

It wasn't just me.

I really looked forward to our times together.

Mrs. Hazel didn't bake anymore, so I would make sure that we stopped by the bakery to pick up some pastries at her request, which she would complain wasn't good for her health, as she consumed them without leaving any crumbs.

I had last spoken to her on Mother's Day. I called to wish her a happy celebration and sent some flowers to her. Then, one day I called and her line didn't ring; there was only this weird buzzing sound each time I dialed her number. I tried reaching her several more times that morning, but the call still wouldn't ring through.

My heart sank, but I was thinking that maybe she had gone to the hospital. She had always had trouble breathing, especially through her later years. At least, that was what I wanted to believe, but I knew better.

I could feel that there was something odd about it all.

This odd feeling had been going on for weeks now, yet I had been too busy with work, and blamed it on the stress. My instincts pushing me, I 'googled' her name and instantly fell to my knees.

Hazel P. Crump; African American female
Died May 22, 2017

Mrs. Hazel had passed away a month or so prior, and I had not been there.

It was devastating for me. She was my best friend, and had really been there for me when I was a child. I have cried off and on for months, and although the pain still remains fresh, I know she's in a better place.

I wish I had done more for her, but I am grateful that I had cared for her, and been there when she needed me.

At 89 years old, she had lived a beautiful life; filled with so much kindness. I don't think she truly had an idea of how much she helped me.

Sadly, the world misses out on her kindness, which I was opportune to be a recipient of.

Hers was indeed a life, well lived.

> **"The purpose of life is not to be happy, it is to be useful, to be honorable, to be compassionate, to have it make some difference that you have lived and lived well."**
> ~Ralph Waldo Emerson

That is a quote that details the life of my next *lifeline*, "Liz", who was one of the neighborhood prostitutes I met getting off of the school bus one afternoon.

Back then, I really had no clue as to what her life entailed, but I was smart enough to know that she knew an awfully large number of different colored males.

The older kids would tease at her, but I was never too fond of bullying. I remember this day like it was yesterday, because I was going to beat the brakes off of this kid for bothering her. She would occasionally wait for me to get off the school bus in the evenings to put money in my hand; making me promise to not end up like her.

I can recall the first time it happened.

As she walked up to me in heels so high, I could only wonder how she managed to strut so confidently without any wobbling; especially now that I wear heels as an adult woman. Her hair was bleached blonde, with dark roots showing, and she was wearing a short gown that barely covered her tights. She stopped right in front of me, and with a smile that showed a mouth full of white teeth, she stretched her hand out.

"Take this, little Ebony," she said.

Shocked, I had no idea how she even knew my name. Sure, we lived in the same neighborhood, but that was the first time our paths had ever crossed, although I had heard about her from the neighborhood gossips that were worse than present day TMZ.

This tradition of hers continued for a very long time, and I have to admit, I was looking forward to the money I was getting from her, and saving it under my bed. Once it had amassed into a substantial sum, I would either use it for my needs, usually basketball shoes, or hand it over to my mother.

There was a time it had increased to $100, and another time, it went higher than that. I saw past her shield to how fragile she was, but her choice of livelihood was a necessity for her; it was what she thought she knew how to do best.

We didn't talk much, to be honest, and whenever we did, she always led the conversation. She was pretty, with big eyes and full lips, and she always had that sad, longing look in her eyes. It made me want to hug her because I knew it wasn't easy for her; however, I didn't know if it was going to make her uncomfortable.

At times, when she was in a conversational mood, she would sit at the sidewalks and pat the ground for me to join her. We could sit in silence for a while, or she would ask about schoolwork and what I was up to.

Liz would not let me leave until I made a promise to continue going to school, excel in my studies, and not work the streets like her. She was technically a stranger to me, but she wanted me to prosper; something she had failed to achieve.

The kids in the neighborhood would pick on her. However, I made it my business to defend and talk to her; ignoring the annoyed looks the other kids threw at me. They didn't like her? Well, that was their business, not mine. I remember a time we were on the street playing double-dutch, and she walked past with a black eye; clutching her bag. I could hear the other kids snickering.

I glared at them, yet they continued.

So, I went right after her, and although I can't remember what we spoke about, there was a bright smile on her face when she went on her way.

The game had ended when I returned to more glares from the other kids. I just glared right back at them.

See, I wasn't here for bullying. I didn't mind being the sacrifice for others. She was a white female, and kept herself together. I don't think I saw her speaking to anyone else, aside from me, and each time we spoke, it was on the street. Even the adults treated her in an aloof manner; talking about how she was a high class escort or prostitute.

All I knew, is that whenever she placed money in my hand, she would say, *"You're different, little lady. Promise me that you won't end up like me."*

There was so much good in her.

She didn't owe me any form of obligation, and I didn't ask to be the recipient of her kindness; however she, out of the kindness of her heart, decided to support me in her own little way.

My mom told me that she saw her about five years ago, and she's doing very well. According to ma, she could barely recognize her, because she looked different... in a positive way.

I was glad to hear this. It is a total life change for her, one I believe she really deserves. I haven't been able to find her, but I hope I do so someday.

The mediocre teacher tells. The good teacher explains. The superior teacher demonstrates. The great teacher inspires."
~William A. Ward

The neighborhoods I grew up in were poverty stricken; however, my mom would find the better neighborhoods on Section 8. We moved to Dearborn Drive when I started 5th grade, and my 5th grade teacher, Carolyn Young, was the right one for us Bae Bae's kids.

I remember when I met her for the first time; tall, high-yellow, gorgeous short cut, and intelligent. I had never encountered someone so smart and well spoken.

She was classy, witty, hilarious, and she did not play. She was straight to the point, and barely flashed a smile in class. The other kids were in awe of her, stepping out of her way immediately when they spotted her, the boys had huge crushes on her, and she left them stunned in their words, while we girls wanted to be classy like her.

I tried to dress and walk like her, but it only made me feel ridiculous. I was told by my friends that they had tried to do so as well, but had given up. Even the other teachers treated her with much respect and I knew from gossips that they didn't want to get on her wrong side.

She was stern, but she had an amazing personality and aura; able to carry everyone involved along.

If Ms. Young was in charge of a project in school, everyone wanted to sign up because they knew how good it was going to be, due to her diligence and creativity.

I loved her classes a lot, as I was always captivated for the duration of it. Kanesha, a friend of mine who had a carefree attitude, especially towards her education, always tried to act like she was unaffected. Still, I would catch her with her eyes rooted on Ms. Young as she spoke; her captivating voice filling the room.

I used to think that our school didn't deserve her intelligent mind. She just seemed out of the world with her approach towards educating us. It was as if the other teachers had attended a rundown community college, and she had come from Harvard.

Well, one day in particular my classmates and I decided that we would torture her. I guess we wanted to see her fall off the high pedestal everyone had placed her on. How was she going to react? Would it make her more homely? We had tortured most of our teachers in one way or another. There was a time we hid all of our English teacher's books, and for the rest of the day, we helped her look for them. However, Ms. Young's torture was going to be more serious than the others we had tried in the past.

It was like the scene from **Sister Act** where Whoopi was glued to the chair, but without the glue. We gave her pure hell that day and even did the ultimate NO in her classroom. Anything she said, we did the opposite. "Bring out your books," and we kept them right in our bags.

Someone brought a stereo and we began to dance, some of us even doing ballet poses.

Nothing she said, or did could make us stop.

Under my leadership, we were on a roll, and we could only get worse. However, at some point in my being a complete nuisance that day, I became convicted. Seeing her look so disappointed in us, unnerved me. I had never seen her so out of control; her demeanor shattered. All she had tried to do was help us, and we had repaid her in such an ungrateful way.

How could we treat her so mean, and misbehave so terribly when she loved us so much?

Well, I felt bad and I started a letter of apology.

Then, we ever so carefully had every classmate sign it. By the time she noticed that we were passing a note around in her class, we had all signed it. I could see the disbelief on her face as she read the letter quietly, but she also showed a flattered type of joy.

How we had slipped this by her was the questionable look on her face, and who had started it? It was me... and Ms. Young told me to wait behind after class.

From that day, she took me under her wing.

I had always admired her, but never did I ever imagine that she would have a personal interest in me. She mentored me in my schoolwork, and it was like I had a private teacher of my own. She also taught me lessons of becoming a little lady, and we would spend some of our time together talking about life in general.

One day, she picked me up from my home. She came to meet my mom and she looked right at home as we all talked in the living room. Afterwards, she took me to the movies to see Jurassic Park. I remember everything about that day, even down to the partially wet jumper set that I wore because the heater didn't dry it all the way.

My friends teased me about how I had become a teacher's favorite, and they wanted to hear all about her.

In my own way, I was closemouthed about her, wanting her all to myself.

When I look back, it is indeed a miracle how everything just fell into place without my even doing much. All we wanted was to tease our teacher, and instead, I got a lifelong friend who has made a huge impact in my life. From that day forward, I wanted to make Ms. Young proud. I would go the extra mile in reading so that in class, I was prepared to answer her questions; I didn't want to disappoint her in any way.

Whenever I messed up, she didn't hesitate to call me out, and suggest ways I could make amends. She became another *lifeline* for me when I was drowning, without even realizing it. As a matter of fact, she saved my life. Her genuine love as a teacher and mentor provoked me to want to learn and I have never stopped.

She had a high standard of what she expected for me, and I have worked hard all through the years to surpass that standard; to tell her that, "I did it".

She continues to be one of my greatest supporters, and every major event in my life she was with me; clapping and rooting for me.

Ms. Young is my SHERO.

> "She simply touched her
> with her wand, and at the same moment, her
> clothes were turned into cloth of gold and silver,
> all decked with jewels."
>
> ~ Charles Perrault

In my eleventh grade year, I began dating a young man. I was a kid who thought I was in love, but I think I was more after the thought of being loved and protected.

However, it wasn't him I needed; it was his mother that I needed most at that time in my life. She was indeed my *lifeline*. She poured into me and showed me a love that constantly made me better.

How I dress to this day is a testament of how she and my godmother, Tyressa McCormick, showed me what class truly is. I remember walking into church one day with a spaghetti-strapped dress on. I was tiny and cute, but I naturally demanded attention when I walked into a room; and, I still do. So, I was strutting and relishing in all the attention like I was the Queen.

After dinner that night, Mrs. Trudie, my boyfriend's mother had a long letter waiting for me. She was not tearing me down, but rather, showing me how to carry myself as a lady; especially in the house of God.

She helped me to identify with the *"Three Times a Lady"* that I've become. And, though I don't get dressed with people in mind, I was aware that I had to remember that I had somebody holding me accountable; which has given me the understanding that somebody cared, somebody is watching. I can't let her down because of all that she had poured into me.

A couple of years later, when I got sick in college and I had to have surgery to remove fibroid tumors that were pressing against my ovaries, Miss Trudy and Greg's father came, picked me up from the campus, and took me to the hospital. But, the thing was… I didn't have any insurance.

So, Miss Trudy and her husband set up a payment plan with the hospital; taking care of whatever the initial payment was, as well as paying off my hospital bills. I don't even know what that cost them. This is why I have always felt indebted to prove to her that their labor and love for me was not in vain.

Now my Godmother, Tyressa.

To know her is to instantly fall in love with her. Hilariously funny, but a woman of genuine love, integrity, and a preaching machine. Tyressa, took me under her wing at the church my mother joined. This was the church where I sang on the praise team, and served on the Jr. Highways and Hedges board, TOT Choir, etc.

I loved God, but the promiscuous nature that I believe developed from molestation made me a WHOLE "HOE".

I was humping my *whole* life away, and every time I think about the fact that I didn't contract HIV and other STDs, I give God praise for how much He protected a lost me.

My childhood friend/sister "Tinkerbell" and I were dating two brothers, Moses and Louis. My God, today and tomorrow, they were drop dead gorgeous. Although I was a "hoe saint", I loved God, and I was big on inviting my friends to church. On this particular Sunday, Moses came to church on my invitation, and after service I was just so utterly proud to introduce him to my godmother. She looked at him and said, *"Hi son, what's your name?"*

"Moses," he answered, with a meek smile.

"Okay Moses. Just make sure that you're not trying to part my baby's red sea," my godmother said blankly; without any hint of a smile. He turned red and I just stood in disbelief. Shortly after, he dumped me, and I haven't seen his fine self since.

Thanks "god-mom."

So, now that you've met some of those special individuals who have operated as lifelines in my life; shaping and molding my thought processes, behaviors, and belief systems, and without whose presence in my upbringing, I would have never made it through childhood into who I would one day become, let me introduce you to "Three Times a Lady".

... *The Woman. Her Business. Her God.*

The Woman

"Sometimes, it is hard to see the rainbow when there have been endless days of rain."
~ Kristina Greer

Life is such an amazing journey, filled with ups and downs. Even when you think you have it all figured out, you will be surprised to find hurdles which you never did anticipate. But then, that's just how life works.

My mom, Lalonnie Rankin, and my dad, Dalton Jones, were around 16 or 17 when they got pregnant with me. My mom's parents had moved to Kinston, North Carolina, and my parents had met through my grandfather, William Ormond, who had been a Chief of

Police in New York. He had a singing group at the time, and my father used to sing with this group.

I've been told that my grandfather was going to kill my daddy for getting my Mom pregnant, and since he was a police officer in Kinston, as well, I believe that he could have made it happen!

Nevertheless, despite my grandfather's attempts to shield his family from poverty and violence, my uncles were some pretty tough cats and had begun getting into a lot of different things that immediately started to plague the career of my grandfather.

So, he uprooted and moved to Durham.

This is how I ended up living with my grandmother for the first few years of my life.

Then, from what I've heard this one particular weekend, my Momma had asked if she could take me to Durham for a family gathering; promising to bring me back afterward. My Grandma was hesitant at first, but then after speaking with my dad, agreed to let her take me, as long as she brought me back.

But, she didn't.

For the next few months, no one could find me; they had no idea where I was. Until one day, almost a year later, my grandmother and father just happened to run into a family member, who told her where we were. The two of them immediately jumped into the car and took off toward Durham to find me.

And, that they did.

They found me, at five years of age, living in less than favorable conditions in the Bragtown Projects, sleeping on a bed that was basically just the box spring; only a thin quilt separating the sharp metals coils and me.

My momma hadn't enrolled me in school, nor had I even been to kindergarten yet. my Uncle Billy and Aunt Net *and* their kids had also moved into this small apartment. This was long before my Mom had gotten saved. It was crazy, but it was the norm for the environment at that time; parties, drugs, drinking, fighting, and anything else you can imagine was going on.

My mom, her brothers, cousins, and a few Aunties were all living in Bragtown at the time and we ran that place. Not just my Uncles, but my Mom and Aunts too.

I've seen my Mom literally drag women, nearly stomping a mud-hole in them. She too was a fighter. She too had been molested. She too had never healed, and if you crossed her wrong, you immediately would see the female version of the hulk.

My mother did not play and I thought I was just as bad as she was. Seeing my family fight and carry on, even witnessing my mother get stabbed, were memories that I knew I couldn't relive in my personal life.

Over time, I had begun having really bad seizures. Many, stemming from the chaos that surrounded us... Police sirens, gun shots, you name it and I've experienced it. I remember my dad would cry all the way back to Kinston whenever they would pick me up, due to the circumstances they had found me in. So, from that point on, every holiday, every birthday, summer vacation, I don't care what it was - it could have been Valentine's Day - my daddy was coming to Durham to get me.

Now, let's be very clear, I never want my Momma to be portrayed as a bad parent, because it really wasn't like that. I honestly believe, and I'm not making excuses for her, that she gave me what she had to give. Therefore, I cherish every moment with her and love her for who she is and for who she raised me to be. Even with little, she gave me more than she could probably afford to at the time. I'm her heartbeat and she makes that known. If nothing else, I can say that my mother loves me.

She admires me, and that's big.

Nevertheless, being able to see both sides, to live with both the good and the negative, caused me to want more out of my life; to dream bigger than what I saw.

I've always been athletic, even when I was younger. So, when my daddy came to get me, he would take me to the arcade to play games. I also began playing basketball, which is what kept me out of the streets. Every summer I played ball with my cousins on a dirt court that only hosted a swing set.

We tore the bars out of the monkey bars and that was where I developed my lethal 3-point shot.

I was, and still remain, a beast on the court. Basketball had become my way of escape. Well, that and going to church with my grandmother. I can still remember laying my head on her lap while she played the piano during services as a child.

I would go from that environment of prayer, church, love etc., back to Durham with all of the craziness.

Neither Gawmaw nor my dad had much. They didn't have money to go to court and fight for legal custody of me; however, they had a lot of love for me. And, people were always putting money in my hands. Even my daddy, who earned his money from his lawn care business, would come home sometimes from cutting grass all day, and just sit handfuls of money onto my lap.

There was always somebody that God would send to just bridge the gap between poverty and supply the necessities of life. Like, around the time in my junior year in college I needed a few dollars to get something to eat and my Pastor's nephew, who was a big time drug dealer, told me to go into his closet and get the funds I needed out of one of the bags that were in there.

See, I always had access to money. It was attracted to me and I was in love with it. I stopped by my homeboy's house and told him what I needed.

He kept bags of money in the water heater closet and he would just let me get whatever I needed out of it. I would stick my hands in the bag and pull out stacks of cash. That was the norm of our relationship, until this one time when I had come home from college and gone to the park to play ball. We ended up leaving the basketball court early because a few of my homeboys had gotten into a fight and begun shooting at one another.

I remember running towards my little brother and having to jump a fence to keep us from getting shot. I thought the day was crazy enough, but when I got to my homeboy's house and knocked on the door, he wouldn't let me in. He kept saying, *"Naw Eb, you can't come in."* I nagged and nagged him, and eventually he opened the door; pulling me inside forcefully.

He grabbed my shirt and pulled me to the back door. When we reached the back glass sliding door, he handed me a pair of binoculars and told me to look out of them.

When I looked into the binoculars, to my surprise, the Feds were starring back at me. The FBI had been investigating them for a murder and for the massive drug ring that they had going on.

He looked at me, handed me a wad of cash from the closet, and told me to promise to stay my "ass" in school.

The next week, my Mom called me at college to tell me that the Feds had busted that house and that all of my homeboys had gotten locked up. All I could think about was *what would have happened if the Feds had run up in the house while I was there?*

That situation provoked me to have a mindset of being responsible for the mentees who would come later on in my life. Those I had no idea about yet.

Tony Peaks was a drug dealer, but that drug dealer helped to change my life. He was killed in Durham a few years ago.

I'VE GOT CONFIDENCE

Many are in a comatose state as they have limited what could become of themselves. The truth of the matter is that "life has many things to offer, but you have the authority to determine for your life what is accepted."

This is a context that has been neglected by many. Some do not even have the control of their lives any longer; they have given the circumstances of life to be the driver of their lives.

It is painful to see that confidence in so many has lost its value and "when you fail to have self-assurance in yourself the quality and certainty of you, and that which you dreamt to be will become void".

If we were to poll my friends, Nedra Hill, Derica Gaston, Kristen Green, Shamira Green (Resting In Heaven) , any of them, they would approve my role in their lives as their outspoken voice. It literally makes me cringe when I see others being taken advantage of.

I don't think that I really understood the damage of what was done to me in my youth, until the last miscarriage with my second set of twins. That anger was manifesting in every form possible. The opportunity to protect anything, whether it was myself, my brothers, my Momma, or my friends, I leaped at it. It reminded me of how I wanted someone there to protect me.

I became angry.

Now this is the thing, as sweet as you may probably think I am, I am even feistier. I never backed down and I could destroy a pigeon's will to fly with my witty smart mouth. I was a pure fireball growing up and in some ways, I still am.

There was always a fighter in me, literally.

Reflecting back, this was anger pinned up from the molestation. I had made the decision a long time ago that no one else was going to get over on me. I had assured myself that history would not repeat itself, and that I would always be shielded; ready for war.

I lived like Steve Harvey. Say something to shock me and I'll shock you back. I became a fighter and it didn't matter my size versus yours, my age versus yours.

I did not care. If you wronged me, I didn't even wait for an apology, I was ready to wage war on you like a thousand battalions. I chased a friend for a mile and a half down the street with a butcher knife for bothering my brother. I jumped on my bus driver for bothering me and my brother. I pushed a girl through a glass door when she spat on me and attempted to run, not knowing that I was a pure athlete. When I caught up with her, the look on her face gave me pure bliss.

Once, I dragged a girl down the stairs at church when she thought that she was bad enough to slap me; not caring that my elders were looking on. All I wanted was to get even and for her, and others, to be aware that they couldn't cross me and get away with it.

My handprint was left on my cousin's face for drinking my Kool-Aid. I stabbed my uncle when he acted like he was going to fight my little brother; he was being all crazy, yelling obscenities and puffing his chest out.

The same uncle pulled a gun out on me when I jumped on him for bothering my cousin. A knife was my friend. It was anger, because I wanted to kill my abuser.

I said all of that, to say this... in spite of it all, there was still something within me that would not let me allow the enemy to get a hold; I wasn't going to be tormented. I wasn't going to lose my mind.

There was no way I was going to let that be *the end*.

It wasn't going to happen.

This fight, probably a result of my childhood, causes me to push women to have a voice. Mine often gets me into trouble, but I'd rather be heard loud and clear than to suffer in silence from a lack of effective noise.

When you give no place to confidence in you, then fear will be in control of your life.

I tell you this,

*"If you are not self-motivated,
you cannot be stricter with your determination."*

You can only produce the best of what you are by encouraging yourself. Nothing in life comes to reality just by theory or imagination. Sure, you can have a big dream and ideas to accomplish a purpose, yet that which you have in your brain can only come to reality by the practical; and that is where self-assurance comes in.

It would be a waste of time deliberating, dreaming, or having loads of ideas without having faith in *you*.

Stagnancy will always be the state of a man, or woman) who refuses to disregard the fear of becoming a failure. Have you been thinking that failure is measured by the mistakes you committed? If you give in to such, it will only make you useless and not able to come out with something great.

No, it is wrong to have such perspective.

Your confidence, and your faith will build your dream.

"You will only become a failure if you refuse to make your mistakes a stepping stone to your greatness."
~ Ebony O.H.

In the quest to developing confidence, trust, and faith in yourself, there are so many traps and pitfalls; however, these should not distract you from the focus.

One of the things that will cause your confidence to be elevated is persistence. Still, to be clear, your priorities need to be right. If you set your priority wrongly, it will only yield to disaster. If you are a kind that believes in your God; God has to be your greatest priority, while other things that are important to you will follow.

If you are living a life without focus on right priorities, well then, you need to get that straight, but above all else embrace you, love you, and by all means have confidence in you.

THE MISCARRIAGES

Who can actually survive twelve miscarriages and not lose their mind? The loss of 14 babies (12 pregnancies with 2 sets of twins) has been very tough for me.

I don't think any words written can convey how much pain and torment they indeed were. It's a mother's joy to have a child, and to watch her child grow within her. Then what happens, when she loses her precious baby? Not once, not twice, but over and over again; like a broken record. It was an unimaginable ordeal for me, one I would like to wish never happened, but God works in mysterious ways.

The first miscarriage occurred in late 2003, when Andre and I were dating. We had been dating for almost a year when I found out that I was pregnant. We were very excited, and I didn't care what sex our baby was going to be. A boy or a girl, I promised myself that I would be the best mother ever, and to always be there for my child.

Little did I know what was ahead...

We had gone home to Kinston, to visit our families and to tell my grandma that I was pregnant. I remember that I had started cramping really bad, but we thought it was just part of the whole pregnancy thing or that I had overdone it with the long four-hour drive from Winston-Salem to Kinston.

Therefore, we went on to see Andre's mom.

I always enjoy spending time with his mom. Our relationship has always been amazing; with her responding to me as if I were her child. You cannot tell her that I'm not her daughter. Most wife and Mother-in-law stories are something similar to "The Devil Wears Prada", but not with us.

That's my Momma.

So, when she saw me in so much pain, she immediately began to tend to me by purchasing a heating pad and personally doing whatever she could to make me comfortable. And you know, we finally ended up telling her that I was pregnant.

As it was getting late in the evening and the pain wasn't abating, Dre decided to take me back to my grandmother's house. Because no matter how old I was, my grandmother didn't play that whole staying the night at a boy's house kind-of-thing... And so, we returned to grandma's, and she was across the street playing 1500 (spades) with her sisters.

I went into the house and sat down on the couch to rest, when she came in to see about me. I remember telling her that I was hurting badly, and she just looked at me for a moment; concerned, yet not pressing the issue.

She had this look like she was just waiting for me to confirm that I was pregnant.

However, by this time, the pain had only increased. Thinking that I just needed to use the restroom, I weakly walked to the bathroom; hoping that the terrible discomfort would soon be over. Unfortunately I was wrong, and no sooner than I sat down on the commode, a baby dropped into the toilet.

Screaming, I called out for help.

Immediately, Andre and my grandma came in, and as soon as she realized what had happened, my grandmother grabbed a towel and placed the baby in it.

Everyone, myself, Dre, grandma, *and* granddaddy, were in total shock.

The ambulance was called, and I began having one of the worst panic attacks I had ever experienced in my life. I was losing so much blood...

Once the paramedics arrived, the house quickly grew loud with relatives trooping in and out; all in a bid to get a grasp of the situation. They were giving me their sympathies, but I knew some of them secretly loved and relished my misfortune. Even a few nosey relatives popped in to see if this was really happening, one of them saying, *"Did Ebony really just disappoint Glenn like this?"* (Glenn was my grandmother's name)

You see, I was her pride and joy. Right from when I was a little girl, she had never hidden the fact that I was her favorite; her baby.

She has always been my number one cheerleader – my going into undergrad, after she told it, sounded like I had been accepted into law school; every accomplishment of mine was magnified. I would barely be finished telling her the good news before she was on the phone spreading it to all her relatives, or going down the block telling everyone how I had made her proud.

This kind of genuine love from her afforded me a lot of rolled eyes, and they could get away with it until I got older, and I voiced very boldly how sick I thought they were to be jealous of a grandmother and granddaughter's affection for one another.

So this time, I did feel that I had just let her down. I knew that she was disappointed, as she had really wanted to be a great-grandmother to my child. With all that was going on, my mind was racing. I was in a state of confusion and shock.

I had done things right up to that moment, so I could not understand why I had just lost a baby.

At the hospital, it was clear I had miscarried and that they would need to do a DNC to remove the placenta, so they rushed me into emergency surgery. However, once they were performing the DNC, it became evident that I hadn't lost one baby, but two.

We had lost a set of twins; a little boy and a little girl.

Afterward, I ended up staying in Kinston with my grandmother for a week or so. It would take a while longer for me to get back to any semblance of normal.

Can you imagine that year after year, this was a cycle that continued to repeat itself? I would be successful in getting pregnant, carry my child up to at least three and four months each time, and then miscarry. It was the worst times of my life and marriage.

It not only devastated me, but broke my husband as well; and unfortunately, he was more worried about his wife and my health than himself; selflessly loving me past the pain and brokenness every single time.

> **"I realized that if my thoughts immediately affect my body, I should be careful about what I think. Now, if I get angry, I ask myself why I feel that way. If I can find the source of my anger, I can turn that negative energy into something positive."**
> ~ Yoko Ono~

Promise Reminder (The Miracle)

The miscarriages continued throughout the course of our marriage, and by now we had joined **Greater**

Tabernacle of Faith, under the leadership of our great Apostle, Brenda J. McCloud; a woman of great faith, influence, strength, class, high fashion, and a prayer warrior indeed.

It was 2010, and Andre and I had experienced 11 miscarriages, with 12 losses. You would have thought I'd lose hope, but the faith that surrounded us and the principles taught to us through prayer and fasting from our leader, kept us believing that God was going to come through on our behalf.

And, guess what? He did!

It was Apostle McCloud who prophesied Sir Cameron Alexander Ham's birth to us before we even knew that I was pregnant. One Sunday, we were sitting in service, and Apostle was up preaching the Word. She stopped and shared a story of how earlier that week she had been watching someone ministering on television.

She said that the woman asked if anyone watching knew of someone barren; someone who was having trouble conceiving. Apostle said she immediately thought of me, and with the number of losses I had endured, I would have probably come to everyone's mind; if they had been asked that question.

Nevertheless, Apostle McCloud immediately went into intercession on my behalf, and I was grateful that she did. I was tired of being embarrassed every year.

For example, Mother's day was dreadful for me.

We would have a rose ceremony every year at the church in honor of Mother's Day, and to ease the pain, Bridget McCloud, my Apostle's daughter-in-law, and Rose Johnson, "Aunt Rose", would buy me a rose in honor of my struggles to conceive and to show that they were believing God with me for my miracle child.

"*Thank you,*" Aunt Bridget and Aunt Rose. If I never said it before, *those roses helped me to not lose my mind. Your roses gave me hope.*" I would be so broken and hurt, but I would have to keep the facade of strength beautifully painted on my face.

That particular Sunday, Apostle had laid hands on me and gave me specific instruction not to travel back to my hometown during this pregnancy.

A few of the miscarriages had happened when I would go back home to Kinston and whatever spirit was lurking didn't need to be presented with the opportunity to attack this pregnancy as well.

We took heed to what our leader said, and out of pure faith and obedience, the day before Valentine's Day, February 13, 2011 at 8:20 p.m., we gave birth to our promise; *our promise reminder*, Sir Cameron Alexander Ham. He was the most handsome little boy that I had ever seen, and despite the fact that I had punched my doctor, gotten wrapped and tied to the bed with surgical tape, and literally put to sleep during his birth, his bright eyes and big smile wiped all of the pain away.

God had kept his promise to me and the faith that I found as a little girl was rebirthed.

Sir Cameron Alexander Ham, better known as "Cam Ham" has been an absolute joy to both me and Andre, as well as everyone else he has come into contact with.

Everything that we asked God for in a child was gifted through our promise. He's witty and very intelligent, with his sense of humor much like Mommy's, and his loving heart and kind spirit much like Daddy's.

He's a natural born singer; it's in his blood... and his love for God is proving to be the most amazing factor of his character thus far. It's no secret that we have birthed a Prophet and a mouthpiece to many nations.

Sir Cameron Alexander Ham: *The Promise Reminder*

Her Business

In 2013, Andre and I made the decision to move our family from North Carolina to Georgia. It had been two years since God had given us our "Promise Reminder", Sir Cameron Alexander Ham, and we wanted more; more than our current life was able to offer us and more than we could give ourselves at that moment.

At the time, Andre had just finished Welding School, and I was in grad school finishing my Master's degree in Public Administration and Leadership. I was on a quest to become a Principal, or so I thought.

I remember going to Apostle McCloud, and telling her that we needed to speak with her. She looked up at me and said, *"I already know. Y'all are leaving."*

Stunned, I couldn't recall if I had shared the information with someone or if the Lord told her, but however it happened, it was all the confirmation I needed to burn the road up.

I knew that my *and* my family's time in the Carolinas had come to an end. It was bittersweet, because my son, even at the age of two, was so in tune and connected to Apostle McCloud; a connection that is unexplainable to this day. He admires, adores, and loves *his Apostle*.

I recall her getting sick one time, and finally being released by the doctors, only to tell the congregation that she wouldn't be able to preach for a while. Cameron was playing on the floor as she shared the news, and when she said, *"The doctors have asked me to sit down. I won't be preaching for a while,"* Cameron blurted out, *"Oh No! That ain't right."*

The entire church was shocked. It was one of those 'out of the mouth of babes' moments, and guess what?

She didn't stop preaching.

Their relationship, I believe, started while Cameron was still in my womb.

So yes, I honestly believe that leaving North Carolina for me was also my way of escaping the pain of my past.

I ministered one time from the subject "I'm Not a Fan of My Past," one of the most inspiring and profound messages I have ever preached. I had enough of the taste.

It was bitter, it was salty, and I refused to allow my past to attach itself to my son.

We ran away to give him a future.

It was June of 2013 to be exact. We loaded up our cars, our two-year-old son, and a U-Haul.

It was over. We were leaving the place where we had become too familiar with poverty; not just financially, but mentally.

> **The only difference between wealth and poverty is a MINDSET.**
> ~Ebony Ormond-Ham

I remember the Lord making it very clear when we arrived in Georgia that we were not to depend on family.

He promised that he would establish us and He did.

The first apartment complex we applied to, we were denied. Well duh... our credit was probably a -654.345 and we didn't have jobs. We literally moved to Georgia with our refund checks from college totaling about $6,000. And, let me share this, I've always been a dreamer, so where we applied to would have eaten up that amount in rent alone.

I bet the Property Manager saw our application and said, "I KNOW YOU LYING." But, I had a promise, so we laughed and journeyed on.

The next place we applied to was called StoneCreek on the Green; more beautiful, high priced apartments that we couldn't afford. In my mind, I was thinking *what's the worst that can happen?* Either they can say 'yes' or 'no', but because of the bounce-back queen inside of me, a *no* only served to fuel my faith.

We walked inside the leasing office to apply and this young, "beautifully-handsome" boy greeted me. He said, *"Oooh you puuuurty"* (pretty). Well, in that moment, I have to say that I used the art of manipulation, flattery, and actually loved to engage in conversation with the young man.

Pause right here, saints.

We do know that manipulation and love don't go in the same sentence right? It's either ministry or manipulation! Anyway, I played the game and I don't know what kind of Tom foolery magic he worked, but he got us approved. Now check this out. He got us approved, gave us furniture from the apartment staging and décor, I mean really dope stuff, and then two weeks later, he quit.

That was the start of our *favor*.

Andre had gotten a welding position through a temp agency and I had received an offer to teach within the Gwinnett Public Schools; however, I knew I wasn't going.

Entrepreneurship was calling my name. It was always there whispering to me, but I didn't have anyone to give it water. My whisper needed water. It needed to clear out all of the trash, clutter, hurt, and disappointments to speak louder to me.

I needed to give it one more try.

God had begun birthing a new level of success and prosperity within me, and it was all attached to Cameron. Success found me when I birthed the promise. All of the other miscarriages in the natural, and physical, were His babies, and I'll just go with the old people saying that "He needed them back", but what He gave me through Cameron was my promise and that couldn't be snatched.

The promise had to live.

Sure enough, miracles one after the other began to flow. The portals of heaven were now open to me.

Why? Because, even if He was through providing for me, He had to take care of the promise...

Excuse me while I dance!

In July, I submitted a proposal to the Center for Medicare and Medicaid (CMS). I'm not sure who received it and how I even got the right email address, but the lady sent it to the owner of Professional Counseling Center of Atlanta. The owner, Larry, reached out to me regarding my purchasing provider numbers that were dormant through PCCA. They had shut the doors to the business.

The offer was initially to sell me the provider numbers; a process starting from scratch that would have taken me two to three years. It sounded great, but where was I going to get $20,000 when we were broke, with no credit, and on food stamps? Here I was again, forced to believe God for the unimaginable, while deep down inside I knew that if nothing else, God had made me a promise that He had to keep.

Two weeks later, Larry had called again to follow up; however, to my surprise, he had a little more to offer.

The Nurse Practitioner, who was in business with Larry and the other PCCA investors, had suddenly taken ill. The offer being presented was rather than purchasing just dormant provider numbers, I would be able to purchase the NP's book of business, and walk in the door with a healthy census.

I remember my heart pounding out of my chest, as I listened to Larry explain the process to me, and encourage me to get the deal completed.

Understand, this now meant that I could literally walk through the door of an accredited Community Mental Health Center worth $2.4 million dollars. Yet, the issue at hand was that I was still on food stamps, broke, and had horrible credit, so there wasn't any chance that I would be able to borrow from a traditional funding institution.

Initially, we needed roughly $20k to purchase, and now I needed a few hundred thousand.

After getting off the phone with Larry, I informed my husband of the conversation, and then, once we had finished talking, I went into my closet and began praying like my Grandmother had taught me.

I reminded God that I had trusted Him, even as a little girl, and that I was certain that there was no way that He would bring this type of opportunity and vision before me without making *provision for the vision.*

Then, I got up from prayer and the Lord spoke to me...telling me to host an Investors Meeting. I was like, *Okay, Lord. But, You do know that I have no earthly idea what an Investors Meeting is, right?*

I kind of smirked at Him, but my faith wouldn't let me sleep. I knew that I had an opportunity to change the direction of my family's life and destroy generational curses of poverty. I started writing an ad that I placed on Craigslist seeking investors to purchase an accredited community mental health center.

About three days later, I began receiving emails from individuals claiming to want to learn more of the opportunity. I reached back out to Larry to inform him of the moves that I was making, and he said to me that if I was able to get the investors to show up, he would fly in from Kentucky to help me seal the deal.

Well, six millionaires showed up to that meeting and Larry flew in, as he had promised.

I walked into the meeting wearing a navy blue blouse and skirt set that I had purchased from JC Penny. It was from the Worthington Collection. I can remember how frightened I was, but even in fear, you would have thought that I had worked in the practice before.

I had done my research; therefore, any terminology that was being presented from a medical or financial aspect, I knew it. Larry was impressed, and the gentlemen continued to chat, and once Larry began his pitch and placed the prior year's financials on the table, everyone wanted in. It was if they were betting on a horse race at the Derby; literally screaming numbers at me, while I sat there in a complete daze.

The guys continued to pitch, trying to convince me why each of them should be my partner, but the Lord drew my attention to this 24-year-old Hispanic millionaire who was quietly waiting his turn to speak.

Initially he wanted to be a silent partner, but I knew that I needed someone with a strong business background and a spirit of integrity. So, as he began to speak, I knew that he was for me: The Right Kind of Help.

Iser helped me to purchase both companies; acquiring 40% ownership. And, after nine months of partnership, I was in a position to buy him out, and have operated as 100% owner ever since.

Yet again, God had kept His promise. Since February 3, 2014, we have been the owners of a very profitable outpatient mental health clinic. This miraculous moment in business is what we started with, but there were also some moments of failure and disappointment.

Twice in owning the company, betrayal hit.

I had a group of clinicians walk out and start their own clinic with the help of my administrative team. And, although it rocked my world for a moment, I knew it was a blessing in disguise. It didn't stop me from growing, expanding, and advancing.

Now, that was what many would call the works of the enemy, but there was also destruction that I caused by being young, unlearned, not too business savvy, and greedy; with a point to prove to everyone who had ever hurt me that I had arrived. There were no more food stamps, and I was driving my dream car.

I was 'stunting' like my Daddy; not being careful or a good steward over what the Lord had entrusted us with.

Debt soon found us, and we owed everybody. The IRS, vendors, you name it. Everyone, except our staff and Landlord, because as frivolous as we were, we understood that we needed our staff to keep the business running, and we also needed a building to operate out of.

Here goes another *lifeline*.

In fact, there were two. Our reimbursements were on hold through our MAC provider, and for nearly two months we were operating on our own funds. We had earned a lot and spent a lot, but we had also saved quite a bit. At this point, everything we had saved was being eaten up, and with an 80k monthly payroll alone, it wasn't hard to run through close to $300,000.

That's exactly what happened.

We had depleted our saving and it was again time for payroll. I remember getting up that morning and making a call to my assistant to inform her that we were going to have to delay payroll. I was so hurt and disappointed in myself and I didn't know which way to turn.

For whatever reason, our landlord called to let us know that he was having a new AC unit put in the building. He and I had developed a pretty good relationship, as I was probably the highest paying tenant at the time in his units, and I had never missed a payment or been late. We began to talk and I informed him that there was a possibility that I would be late with rent.

He immediately took interest in the situation, and then wrote me a check for a very large amount that saved my business, and within eight months, I paid him every dime back. That's the kind of favor that has been on my life, and that's the level of integrity I have learned to display. It has not stopped. I was determined to show him that I was grateful for taking a chance on a young entrepreneur he didn't really know, but bankruptcy and folding wasn't an option.

As I began to take the company in another direction, and revamp the business in order to stimulate revenue, I reached out to my "brother' and friend, Wesley, who has climbed to limitless heights in the industries of banking finance, staffing, and work force solutions.

He too was able to write me a check for an extremely large amount of money, and within a year I had given him back every penny.

Now, the blessing in the two loans from the two individuals that I'm speaking of is that the loans were interest free. This is unheard of in the world of finance; yet quite attainable in the world of *faith* and *favor*.

So, to the current or aspiring entrepreneurs reading this, you don't have any more excuses.

I used them all.

Success is a mindset and it's spiritual. It's a dominant force of victory that can only be stopped by the silencing of your testimony. Had I remained silent from fear of what others would have to say, I would have failed at a business where the blueprint was handed to me.

Had I allowed the enemy to choke me with my failures, I wouldn't have the testimony that Andre and I are on schedule to become completely debt free by 2020; including paying off our home, that was just purchased in August of 2016. God has been faithful to us and we are continuing to climb.

WOMEN AND BUSINESS

Did you know that every third business you encounter is owned by a woman? Yes, one in three businesses is operated by a woman, and they are twice as likely as a man to start their own business.

Owning a business is seen by many women as a way of achieving their financial goals, whilst simultaneously having the flexibility of how those goals are achieved.

At the vanguard of this female entrepreneurial trend are the young; women under 20 are equally likely as their male counterparts to start their own business; whereas, by the thirties or forties, only one in three women will do so. This sounds great, however, female entrepreneurs are only 13% of all the women working; therefore, there is room for more women to embrace autonomy and authority.

The most likely area for women to enter business is the allied health and beauty industries. This equates to jobs like hairdresser, makeup artists, aestheticians, counselor, massage therapist, child care provider, etc.

This tendency comes as no surprise - the idea that women prefer to enter professions that involve close personal contact and care, is in line with the cultural expectations of women, as well as their natural inclinations. If you combine the increasing likelihood of women to start their own business with their preference for 'caregiving' professions, you have a huge army contributing to a more civilized, socially responsible, and egalitarian world.

The number of women in business is rising year by year; and hopefully, you'll join thousands of other women and take seriously the opportunity to develop yourself and contribute to the ever-weaving fabric of human life.

Women are those who make a difference, and with just a little determination and vision, we can matter more than we could have ever imagined.

Women Are Winning

Women are founding companies at a historic rate, with more than 9 million women-owned businesses in the U.S. today. Over the past 15 years, these women-owned firms have grown at a rate 1.5 times faster than other small businesses and are estimated to provide more than 5 million jobs before the end of 2018.

According to the National Women's Business Council (NWBC), the highest number of women-owned firms are in the healthcare, social services, professional, scientific and technical services, admin and retail industries. Interestingly, the NWBC suggests that women start businesses because of limitations in the workforce, personal responsibilities, or the challenges that come from a market that fails to meet their needs.

While women are starting more businesses year after year, their businesses do not appear to grow as quickly or receive as much funding as male-led companies.

A report by The Senate Committee on Small Business & Entrepreneurship highlights current statistics, and offers a "promising new way forward" for women entrepreneurs. The study[1] also reveals a positive picture for women-owned businesses:

- 30 years ago, there were close to 4 million women-owned businesses in the United States. Today, there are over 11 million.
- 39% of all U.S. businesses have women majority ownership, employ nearly 9 million people and generate more than $1.7 trillion in revenue.
- Women are the sole source of income in 40% of all households and outpace men in educational achievement.
- The number of women-owned businesses grew 45% between 2007 – 2016, 5 times faster than the national average
- 78% of new women-owned businesses are owned by women of color.

Even with so much positive news about women-led businesses, in 2016, women received just over 2% of investor and venture capital funding, and women-led businesses made up only 4.9% of VC deals.

---

[1] Senate Committee on Small Business & Entrepreneurship

Obstacles Facing Women Entrepreneurs

The Senate Committee's report focuses on three particularly unique obstacles:

1. Lack of role models and mentors
2. Gender pay gap
3. Unequal access to funding and venture capital

Positive role models inspire and offer guidance to entrepreneurs and small business owners. With media attention on male entrepreneurs, many women lack important motivation that can come from a mentor to inspire them into starting businesses.

The report also noted:

- Adults with mentors are 5 times more likely to say they are planning to start a business.
- 62% of high school girls who are mentored on technology are likely to choose it for a major in college.
- Small business owners who have access to mentoring report higher revenues and growth rates.

The Small Business Administration (SBA) offers access to mentorship for women business owners through

Women's Business Centers, SCORE, and Small Business Development Centers. Women entrepreneurs, with more focus on their successes, can help bring more women into business ownership through mentorship and awareness.

SETTING BUSINESS GOALS

Whether you have small dreams or high potential, setting business goals permits you to design how you want to progress in business. Some accomplishments can take a lifetime to realize, while others can be fulfilled in the sequence of a day.

Regardless of whether you're setting comprehensive primary goals, or planning specific controllable goals towards business, you'll feel a sense of achievement and self-confidence. Getting started can seem discouraging, but you can rise to even the haughtiest dream.

Without defined goals and objectives, your business journey will be a bumpy ride with lots of wrong turns, wasted effort, and missed opportunities. The net result being a negative impact on your profits and business growth (and of course, your stress levels!).

Business goals also play a vital role in shaping your marketing activities. Having clearly defined business goals in place will help you to make important decisions about marketing budget allocation, plan your time efficiently, and keep you focused on your key areas of potential growth.

Without goals, you run the risk of being pulled in multiple directions, taking a reactive rather than proactive approach to your marketing activities; which is never a recipe for success. And, you will be highly unlikely to achieve your full growth and business potential.

To help you with your planning, listed below are simple steps to setting your business goals.

Establish your business goals. Ask yourself some significant questions regarding what you want for your business. What do you wish to accomplish: today, in a year, in your entire business life? Think through what you dream to achieve 5, 10, 15, or 20 years from this time.

A career life goal may perhaps be to open a small home business. A personal goal may possibly be to have a family someday. These goals can be extraordinarily broad.

Split up the big picture into minor and more detailed goals. Ponder on the areas of your business that you either wish to change or that you deem you would like to build up with time. Start asking yourself questions about what you'd like to achieve in each business area and how you would like to approach it within a five year time frame.

Write down business goals for the short term. Now that you identify roughly what you wish to achieve within a few years, make tangible goals for you to start acting on now. Give yourself a target within a logical time frame (surely not more than a year for short-term goals).

- Writing down your goals will make them difficult to overlook, therefore making you responsible for them.
- To start your personal business, your primary goals may be to take an accounting class and to find the ideal location for your bookstore.

Make your business goals small steps that push you towards bigger business goals. In essence, you need to decide the reason you're setting this goal for business and what it's going to achieve. Some worthy questions to question yourself when figuring this out are: does it look worthwhile? Is now the perfect time for this? Does this correspond my needs?

If your answer to the questions is no, think of changing the short term goal to something that is going to be a step towards encountering the set business goal.

Adjust your goals periodically. You may find yourself set in your ways concerning broad business goals, but take the time to re-evaluate your smaller goals.

Are you realizing them rendering to your time frame? Are they still crucial to keep you on track towards your larger business goals?

Allow yourself the flexibility to adjust your goals.

To start your own business, after realizing the first goals of taking an accounting class and finding a location, you may possibly set new goals to acquire a business loan to buy a space and to request for the appropriate business licensing via your local government.

Subsequently, you can move towards purchasing (or hiring) the space, then acquiring the books you need, employing staff, and opening your doors to business.

In the long run you might even work towards opening an additional location!

Having Consistency

By definition, consistency is mostly referred to as adherence to the same principles in a steadfast way. It is a pattern in human behavior, which holds the most important place in every sphere of life. Consistency is the key to success no matter what you are doing.

Personal success is determined by consistency. This is because no relationship can be successful without it. Human beings need consistency in love, hate, friendship, care, and every other human emotion. That is why when you are in a relationship; you would require your partner to be caring, loving, and faithful throughout the life time.

If a partner fails in doing so, the relationship is seriously damaged.

Similarly, consistency in your professional life is also very important. If you are not consistent at work, you are not going to be successful. Consistent performance at work is the only way that is going to get you positive reviews from your bosses and employers.

Consistency in performance is only possible with consistent hard work and dedication. That is why, we see only consistent people in the top managerial positions and in successful entrepreneurial positions.

Consistency is also an essential element of many other things. In your personal business, it is the key ingredient required for success. A business at any scale cannot achieve its goals if it is not consistent in its strategy, planning, and execution. Consistency at this broader level contains even a wider scope.

The main thing that determines the success or failure of a business is checked through the balance in its goal and objectives, and their achievements. Therefore, a business must have the right goals and must consistently review and tweak them for a better future.

Business, whether large or small, cannot survive without consistency. Consistency in performance, research and development, product development, and innovation is required for a better position in the market. In order to keep customers consistently happy, firms need to have a consistent approach towards their operations.

For brands and products, consistency is the ultimate key to success. Research into successful brands from around the world has proven that you don't need a perfect product to be a market leader, but consistent product usually gets the largest share of the market.

This is because customers find it reliable. Customers are much more influenced by the same level of quality and service every time they purchase a product or a service.

It can be very difficult to establish such consistent quality standards, however for successful businesses, it is just the way of doing business. Consistency really works for various products, as it is easy to standardize procedures and processes, whereas for services, it is very difficult to be consistent.

This is because services are usually rendered by humans who can be erroneous. That is why, standardization of services is almost impossible.

Consistency in your business is the key. What are your plans? Do you have set goals that you want to achieve? Set a large, long term goal and then work backwards and set small goals that will get you closer to achieving the larger goal. You will be surprised at the success that this brings to you.

This is a major problem with a lot of people and an issue that many people face in their business. If you are not sure where to turn for help on this subject, get a mentor that has consistency beat. Let them guide you through top strategies for being consistent.

Building Integrity

The single most important standard all new businesses must embrace is a culture of integrity. Perceived misconduct by a business will result in lost customers and a negative reputation that will be difficult to shake. With the proliferation of scammers, con artists, and outright criminals roaming the cubicles of American industry, it is time for business owners to get back to basics. The core of these basics is to develop a culture of integrity that allows your potential customers to rely on your word and commitments, and develop a mutual trust that will allow your business to thrive.

Developing good, mutually beneficial relationships is critical to the success of your business. Dealing with customers, suppliers, and even competitors will be a standard part of your workday, and creating relationships based on trust and mutual respect will matter, especially when you have issues that affect any of those stakeholders.

Now you are probably asking yourself, what is the true nature of integrity? There are in fact some very basic principles that surround the qualities of business integrity. At its core, integrity begins with a company leader who understands the qualities of integrity which then filters down throughout the company into every department and every member's approach and attitude.

Throughout the life of your business, mistakes will be made. Some will be completely your fault (or your employees', which still fall back on you), some will be partly your fault, and some will be not at all your fault, but will still affect your business.

Playing blame-opoly is not necessary, but understanding how the error came about is. That way, you can rework procedures or set standards that reduce the chance of that mistake happening again. People tend to be relatively forgiving, as long as you are up front about the situation and offer solutions to whatever went wrong.

When you know something has gone wrong, let the people that are affected know before they find out another way, and be prepared with either an immediate solution or options for them to choose from. Whatever you do, don't disappear or deny errors.

Take responsibility, and any short-term loss you might suffer will be recovered when you retain those customers and suppliers over the long term.

As the leader in your business, the character you display acts as a guidepost for your employees, as well. Develop a culture that encourages honesty, and you will have far fewer employee issues, better relationships with your customers, and more latitude with your suppliers.

If you receive any reports of your employees behaving in an unethical or dishonest manner, make it clear to them that integrity is a requirement, not a suggestion.

When you come across suppliers or other business associates who are dishonest, find someone else to do business with, if possible.

Small indiscretions that go unacknowledged tend to grow into perpetual mistreatment, especially with individuals who believe that lying to cover an error is acceptable.

As you are developing your business idea into a small business and eventually a thriving company, keep in mind the fallout that comes with a culture of deception; everyone in contact with the situation ends up injured.

Be alert to the culture you and your employees develop, and ensure that all aspects of your business are handled with integrity.

Financial Planning

Over the last few years, we often heard terms like financial planning, personal finance, investment management, retirement planning which have emerged as buzzwords of sorts. Newspapers, blogs, magazines, television channels and just about every one under the sun seem to be talking about the importance of financial planning.

So, what is financial planning? In simple words, Financial Planning is the process of meeting your life goals through the proper management of your finances. The process of financial planning should help you answer questions; such as:

- Where are you today? That is, your current personal balance sheet,
- Where do you want to be tomorrow? That is, finances linked to your goals, and
- What you must do to get there? That is, what you must do to reach your goals.

Financial Planning provides you with a method for organizing your financial future, so that you can plan for the unforeseen. Organizing your finances empowers you to be independent and handle unpredictable events in your life. Successful personal financial planning is crucial for anyone who wishes to manage financial difficulties and accumulate wealth.

Developing a financial plan needs a consideration of various factors. This includes client's current financial status, their financial goals, any outstanding loan, investment instruments, insurance requirement, retirement corpus, inflation, risk profile, tax liability etc.

The process involves gathering relevant financial information, setting life goals (such as children's education, buying a home, buying a car, etc.), examining your current financial status, and coming up with a strategy or plan for how you can meet your goals given your current situation and future plans.

So, why is financial planning important? Listed below are some of the importances of financial planning.

- It helps in increasing cash flow, as well as, monitoring the spending pattern. The cash flow is increased by undertaking measures such as tax planning, prudent spending, and careful budgeting.

- A proper financial estimate/plan that considers the income and expenditure of a person, helps in choosing the right investment policy. It enables the person to reach the set goals.

- It helps gaining an understanding about the current financial position. Adjustments in an investment plan or evaluating a retirement scheme becomes easy for an individual with financial understanding.

- Providing for your family's financial security is an important part of the FP process. Having the proper insurance coverage and policies in place can provide peace of mind for you and your loved ones.

- It helps you to achieve financial freedom; enabling you to meet financial goals and obligations.

Now, let's highlight things you have to do if you are going to take control of your financial future. Remember, without disciplining yourself to do these things, you will not have the chance of achieving your financial plan, because controlling yourself is the most important aspect of your financial planning.

1. **Forget about it:** What ever happened in the past is gone, so *just forget about it*. Money is described in financial circles as being a "liquid asset", which indicates that it has all the characteristics as water. Therefore, as water spilled on the ground

cannot be gathered up again, so it is with money wasted. Move forward.

2. **Start Now:** Forget about yesterday, but begin today to take control of your money. While you cannot change yesterday, you can greatly impact your tomorrow. Never forget that it is not money that builds wealth - it is time. By not starting now, you are throwing time away; and you cannot afford to do that.

3. **Get Committed:** Your financial freedom makes a huge difference in the quality of your life, yet it is created not by one huge thing, but by doing lots of little things *right* over a long period of time. Doing the little things take commitment. Never forget that all success, whether in business, in relationships, or in life, comes at the end of the road of commitment!

4. **Put It In Writing:** If you are not setting specific financial objectives, and implementing a workable plan in writing, then you are setting yourself up for disappointment. Are your financial goals in writing? Do you have a step-by-step action plan that will lead to your financial success?

4. Stop over Spending: The cost of your undisciplined spending is your financial future. Your money is a resource that must be conserved and focused on your goals. Anything less is wasteful. Never forget that every dollar you spend has the potential for jeopardizing, rather than enhancing, your future.

6. Control your Time: There is no question that money is a scarce resource; however, an even scarcer resource is your time. So, you need to guard it zealously and make sure that you are always using it for your maximum benefit. Also, do not fall into the trap of believing that time is money. *No way...* Money mistakes can be corrected, but time mistakes can never be corrected. Once you have lost time, it is gone forever.

7. Control your Risk: Never allow yourself to be blinded by the returns of an investment, by remembering that the key to making money is not to lose it. And, it is always better to grow your money slowly, than to look for quick gains.

You may not realize it but the most important aspect of financial planning is you. That is right it all about you!

And, while there may be some financial things you have to do, it all comes down to you.

And your financial success or lack thereof is predicated on your ability to understand and make informed and effective decisions about the use and management of your money.

Millionaire Mindset

One of the biggest things that holds people back from making the money they want, whether it is online or offline, is having the right mindset. This is, without question, the most important thing to have, and something people spend tens of thousands of dollars acquiring through expensive training programs and audio books.

But, what is this mindset and how do you get it? Can you learn the millionaire mindset and apply it to your life, so that you literally think yourself rich?

Yes, you can.

This mindset isn't something you are born with, but it is something you learn and develop as you go through life. A lot of it is about how you interpret the events that happen to you. For example, you can use events in your life as positive things that build you up, or negative things that drag you down.

If you ask yourself "Why me?" or "Why do bad things always happen to me?" or similar questions when bad things happen in your life, then you are going to find yourself not developing the right mindset.

Having a wealthy mindset comes from asking yourself questions and interpreting events so that they *build you up* and *re-inforce* positive behavior. Look for the positive in everything that happens to you and you will find it.

Admittedly, sometimes you have to look hard, but it is there and you will find that this attitude will help you be more successful and create the mindset of wealth.

But it's more than this; you have to literally program yourself for success. Why do you think the book *"Think And Grow Rich"* is found on the shelves of many of the world's most successful people? Is it because it looks good and they like to pretend they are educated?

No... it's because it works and the information in there is not only valuable, but effective too!

Programming yourself for success, whether using a book or another method is one of the big secrets. You need to program yourself to look for, recognize and take advantage of the opportunities life presents you, which is where many people struggle. They are so focused on making money and getting rich that they don't see all the opportunities being presented to them.

Until you are able to produce the results you desire through your own thoughts and actions, you have only set yourself up to be dependent on other people's thoughts and actions.

This, my friends, will NEVER get you to achieve a Millionaire Mindset for Entrepreneurs. Listed below are some distinctions between what is and what isn't.

1. Thoughts vs. Actions: It's great to have goals and even better to have intentions. A goal will continue to give you something to think about and an intention will give you something to start taking action on. Positive thinking with no action leaves you in the same place you were before you started thinking...on the couch dreaming! If your actions are not in line with your thoughts and vice versa, you will end up wondering why you aren't getting the results you're after. Make a thought an intention and then go do it!

2. Accountability vs. Blaming: Developing a Millionaire Mindset for Entrepreneurs sometimes means you have to take it on the chin from time to time. You see, you're not going to get very far if you continue to take the easy road. And, when you decide to take the road less traveled, sometimes you make mistakes or try to take short cuts. Face it, you're going to screw up. This is a part of learning and growing. What matters is what you do when you screw up. If you say things like, "You said I should..." or "You made me do this..." then you have a long road ahead of you. On the other hand, the sooner you take accountability for your actions and your results, the quicker you will get to where you're headed. You are where you are because of YOU!

5. **Leading vs. Following:** Do you find yourself always agreeing with the crowd? Do you try and talk friends and colleagues out of an idea? If this fits your personality, you are a follower. You need to start being the person who makes claims and believes that there are bigger and better things waiting for you. Don't worry about the people in your life who say things like, "C'mon, that stuff doesn't really happen" or "Maybe you should take the easy way first before you go for it." DO NOT let these people's nervousness and weakness affect your mindset. Just because these people are afraid doesn't mean you should be. In fact, this is the perfect time for you to be a leader and show them it IS possible and there is nothing to be afraid of.

Having a Millionaire Mindset for Entrepreneurs is more than just wishful thinking. It is about getting your mind-SET on your intentions and making that happen one way or the other.

When a road block happens, take accountability and go around. When someone tries to talk you out of it, stay focused on your intentions and keep your mind-SET.

Turn those thoughts into actions, and you'll be well on your way to having a Millionaire Mindset.

Conclusion

Women often tend to take themselves out of the game when it comes to business development and promotion. Nevertheless, *success* is truly a very personal and subjective term. Being productive means different things to different people. Though, one common denominator appears to be happiness in some form, and irrespective of the amount of money you make, titles you earn, or values you uphold, it's pretty hard to be happy if you think that no one likes you!

Whether they choose to work inside or outside the home, women often seem to get the short end of the judgment stick, and unfortunately, we women are often the worst offenders when it comes to bashing our own.

Have you ever commented on or criticized the 'soccer moms' and 'helicopter moms' for not being ambitious enough, or the 'working moms' for not being involved enough, or complained that the 'bitchy boss' needs to *get a life*? Women need to support each other, irrespective of priorities and choices, instead of perpetuating negative and counterproductive stereotypes.

In business, successful men are typically seen as confident and assertive, whereas successful women are more often than not considered aggressive and cold-hearted. The stereotype of the 'Angry Boss' stubbornly persists and can be found all around us - it's in movies, magazines, photos, story lines, even in our conversations.

So, why on earth would any girl or woman ever want to aspire to be 'successful' in business, if it means being seen as cold and hard, shunned and resented by everyone around her?

Because we do need strong, confident, and capable women in corporate-level and Board positions; not to increase statistics, or to reflect equal representation, or even to just show them all that women are just as capable as men... Women need to be an integral part of making the decisions and policies that shape the way business can be done and to redefine success.

> **It's a lot easier and faster to succeed
> if you are the one writing the rules.**
> ~ Ebony Ormond Ham

Her God

Grace is further extended to the peculiar and compassionate. It takes a heroic and bold individual to carry out an assignment with the greater reward profiting others in need.
~ Ebony Ormond Ham

IN THE BEGINNING

It is not astonishing that the terms 'peculiar' or 'strange' have been used to detail the characteristics of my personality; even as a young girl. The journey from childhood to adulthood, and the assignments attached to me (alongside my husband Andre), has commenced to paint a clear picture of the destiny that lies ahead.

I've always had an instinctive desire to know God... to truly know Him. I would say this began with me tagging along to church with my grandmother, who is a pianist for a few churches, from the time I was about three or four years old. **Rouses Chapel**, one particular church that she played for back then, further helped me to develop a deeper knowledge of God. As my grandmother would play, I would sit on the piano stool with her, falling asleep, while she just laid me across her lap and continued playing.

This was how my spiritual journey was sparked.

And, since I was often left in the care of this woman of faith and integrity, there were many opportunities for her to pour her values and principles into me; the greatest of these being prayer. There was never a night that would pass without my grandmother having me on my knees to pray! I can still vividly remember being so shy and not wanting to do so. I would whine and sob about not knowing how to pray like her, and she would look at me sternly and quote the scripture saying, *"If you are ashamed of me before men, I will be ashamed of you before my father."*

As a child, the scripture alone would put fear in me, which is where prayer really started for me. I would try to regurgitate what my grandmother had prayed, and this greatly influenced my personal relationship with God, because I had seen my grandmother pray for different things and then saw those things manifest.

My first prayer group began in my grandmother's living room one summer when I was around twelve-years-old. The family owns large sections of land in the area, so there is no one but our family on it, with about three of my grandmother's sisters living around her. She also has first and third cousins nearby; therefore, it would be safe walking the streets at night or going out to visit family. So, a few of my cousins and I would come together at night and sing, chat, pray, and cry for hours.

During one of my summer visits, I was introduced to a kid by the name of Josiah, and his Mom, Mrs. Robin, had recently moved their family to North Carolina on our same street. Mrs. Robin learned of our little prayer group and started taking all of us to church with her.

Going to church with her was amazing, and the members of the congregation were equally amazed that so many young people were coming to church with her who were eager to serve and praise God.

She was indeed a general in the Gospel, and I was intrigued by the anointing she carried.

At that time, I did not know that I also had some gifts of prophecy and discernment in me, which were being nurtured by God.

So, we started meeting in Mrs. Robin's home on the weekends, praying, singing praises, worshiping, and dancing all night long. We would normally begin our meetings around 8:00 at night, and by the time we finished, it would be 4:00 the next morning.

We couldn't wait to be in Mrs. Robin's presence, and although she would teach us about the Bible and Ministry herself, many times she would also call in her ministry friends to witness what was taking place, and they would pour into us as well.

Can you imagine a group of around 15 kids, aged 8 to 15, lying prostrate on their faces and crying out to the Lord through worship? There was nothing God wasn't going to make possible for our obedience and sacrifice to His will for our lives. I really wished someone would have recorded those nights.

When I went back home, I ministered at different churches; usually youth events, Vacation Bible Schools, and so on.

It was around the time I started my first prayer ministry, that my mother was introduced to a ministry in Durham, called **Greater Zion Wall**; pastored by Overseer Viryl Myers and Pastor Terry L. Peaks.

While my mother attended their church, they also utilized me in the various areas of ministry. I was on the youth praise and worship team, as well as a member of the youth choir, which ministered on Friday night live types of services; allowing the youth to speak. They would give us a topic, and we would have to find scripture references and teach the word of God. I remember one night, Overseer Myers anointed me with oil and laid hands on me. She began praying for me, and I fell to my knees, crying, screaming, and hollering out, *"I'm yours, Lord!"*

"I'm yours, Lord."

My body trembling, I knew it was the Holy Ghost. It was the Holy Spirit who had come upon me; like somebody had just set my entire body on fire. I could not stop screaming and crying out.

I had ministered the night before she anointed me, and I remember that she and Prophetess Diane Jackson had both laid hands on me, and Prophetess Jackson spoke a word into my life, saying that *the Lord was going to make my name great, before nations, and before many great men and women.*

Now, I was only around twelve or thirteen. Even then, you could not tell me that God wouldn't do something for me. I have always been a faith-kind of person.

Once I went off to college, my relationship with God became even more solid. The next level of ministry was getting ready to present itself; along with one of the greatest trials I had ever experienced involving a loved one. During my sophomore year in college, I received a phone call that my youngest brother, Anjamont, had been involved in a freak accident in high school.

He was in gym class and they had gone outside for an activity. One of his older friends was leaving school early and as he drove by, my brother and a few of the other kids jumped on the back of the hood of the car.

My brother was thrown from the car, and the impact of hitting the pavement cracked his skull open. Anjamont was in a coma, and they were not expecting him to live.

But God!

The memory of the miracle He had performed for me and my little brother, that time we were without food, ignited a next level of faith for God's supernatural intervention. I found myself tapping into this immortal kind of faith that had me in a daze, as my college roommates drove me to Durham to get to my brother.

I had zoned out, yet I was in a spiritual realm of prayer and faith that had become so natural for me.

When I walked into the hospital, they immediately took me back to see him. That beautiful golden skin and handsome face was barely recognizable. Tears were streaming down my face, but I knew that I was on assignment; God had not brought me and my faith this far, to fail us now. I was his big sister, and it was my job to protect him from the enemy... and I was ready for war with any demon that would present itself.

Nobody, and nothing, was going to get in my way.

My Mom was so distraught that she couldn't handle all that was going on, so I had her give me Power of Attorney to make decisions on my brother's behalf. I put everybody out of the room; *including her*. And, I remember his nurse walking in with a nasty demeanor; one that was going to have her in need of immediate medical attention if she didn't get it all the way together.

For an entire week and a half, I locked myself in my brother's room, and I wouldn't allow any family or friends in; only his doctors. I don't even remember if I slept much because I was praying. Day and night, I would do as instructed by God. I had worship music playing, and I would get in his ear to call his mind and body to line up with the will of God and the prophetic call on his life.

One morning, as I was in worship, I heard him moan. Immediately jumping up, I stood over him and watched as the tears ran down his face. Donnie McClurkin's song, "Again", was playing and I was crying beyond control.

"Again I call you... and again you answer.
Again I need you... and again you're there."

One of my favorite songs to this day.

God had kept His promise to me again. My baby brother was out of the coma and he was starting to speak. The journey for him has been one that has required much prayer, but the God I serve is faithful.

The Present

Upon my return to college, I was on assignment. My focus was different and I knew that I was on to the next level. My roommate, Shicara Hester, who had also gone to high school in Durham with me, kept me focused.

Her mom had kept her in church as well, so there would be times when I would be in the dorm room, and I would watch Vickie Winans videos every single day.

Back then, I was in love with Vickie Winans. That lady was just so comical and anointed, and for whatever reason, I related to her a lot. Anyway, Shicara would be like, *"Oh my God. Not Vickie again!"*

But, this was the video for the song **"More Than Enough"**, and it just spoke volumes to my relationship with God because I knew him to be just that.

Watching that video almost daily illuminated our dorm room; sparking times of prayer for us. Initially, it was just the two of us praying, and after the word got out, prayer turned into me, Shicara, and four or five other girls praying in our dorm room.

Next thing we knew, the entire second floor of Moore Hall at Winston Salem State University was in the hallway; holding hands and crying out to God.

Soon, the word that we were praying continued to spread, and we went from praying in our dorm room and hallways, to our being afforded the privilege to open Friday night prayer to the entire campus.

That door was opened through one of the Chancellors of student affairs, Mr. Art Malloy.

Our prayer sessions eventually turned into straight church. We had our own musicians, praise team, and fireball preachers like, Kia Hood, who had helped me run the prayer ministry.

It was clear that my steps were being ordered by God; even to my marriage to Andre, which began as a marriage counseling session with my Apostle on a Wednesday night, to our calling friends and family up that same night to inform them that we were having a WHOLE wedding and getting married on Saturday.

Yes, it happened just like that.

We planned our wedding in three days, and my Apostle, Brenda J. McCloud, married us in the company of our loved ones on June 24, 2004.

This is the most hilarious story ever. It was a beautiful little wedding that we didn't even have a photographer for, but I was dolled up in my white wedding gown that cost me $99 at Belk; crowned with a $17 tiara that I played basketball in afterwards at the Fourth of July Park, in Winston Salem.

Andre wore a white suit we had purchased at a buy-one get-one free suit shop, and our wedding reception was literally at the WHOLE park!

That was all we could afford, and we never honeymooned; which was fine with us because sex could happen anywhere.

Amen? Amen!

A prime example that God did a "quick work", this year, on June 24th, we will celebrate 14 years of marriage.

To say the least, His plan for my life was in full affect.

The Newlyweds, Mr. and Mrs. Andre Ham

I began using my pain of the miscarriages to give me an opportunity to birth forth our first conference under my women's empowerment organization, *Three Times A Lady, Inc.*

This conference, named after the testimony of my son, was entitled **Promise Reminder**. Held on January 27-28 at the Impact Church in Atlanta, Georgia, with a total of approximately 1900 attendees for both nights, the *Promise Reminder* conference was keynoted by world renowned and sought after Prophetess Dr. Juanita Bynum.

Later in August, my husband and I launched **The Sneakerhead Youth Empowerment Center**, which is a sneaker design academy for at-risk and special needs youth (sneakerheadyouth.com). My faith could not be shaken. I don't recall a time where I doubted that God was going to come through for me, and although I probably had moments of hurt and pain, I can't ever say that I didn't believe God would provide and give me the desires of my heart.

Determined to not lose focus of the promise, and deciding to continue to trust God for the unimaginable, I made a conscious choice to *use my pain to provoke purpose* in the lives of many women who are trusting God to one day CONCEIVE. The last miscarriage we experienced gained heaven two identical twin girls; nearly costing me my life. In the midst of all the trauma, the doctors lost me twice on the operating table.

The enemy was trying to literally snatch my life. I couldn't even fathom why God would take our girls after he had already fulfilled his promise to us, but that pain birthed the **"I Conceive" Women's Empowerment Weekend.** *"I Conceive"* is a two day event where I will be on-hand to share my inspirational testimony of experiencing (and surviving) 14 miscarriages and nearly losing my life. This is my way of giving back to women who suffer in many areas of life; including fertility, self-doubt, and trauma after emerging from painful experiences and failures.

The Bible declares that *faith is the substance of things hoped for and the evidence of things not seen.* Now, you're talking about faith, which is a non-tangible thing; something you can't even touch. Still, the miraculous might and power of God is able to give substance and value to something without form, through our trust and reliance in him completely.

Reality is, my belief in a power that I can only explain as my mental capacity to believe in or deny the chances of something existing greater than myself, has been the cause of my being alert and in tune with my dreams, goals, and the will of God for my life.

Oprah once asked, *"What is the soul?"*

My answer?

The soul is the part of me that cannot lie, and I believe from my soul, that my alignment with God has positioned me to be *Three Times A Lady;* and to become one with *Myself,* my Business, and my Big GOD!

To Be Continued...

Feminine Financial Quotes

Any powerful and successful woman will tell you that boasting about your accomplishments can cost you. And no, we're not just talking about dollars. Research has shown that women are often discouraged from showing and exhibiting pride in their empires, especially their financial accomplishments and sizeable bank accounts.

Why is this?

Well, it doesn't match up with typical female gender stereotype of submissiveness, interpersonal sensitivity, and supportiveness, for starters.

While they may not be supported culturally in their quest to be rich, that hasn't stopped women all throughout history from discussing their wealth through various quotes about money: its role in their success, how it can negatively and positively affect their lives, and what they're most proud of in regards to their money. But most importantly, these women define money beyond just its dollar amount. It's about independence, opportunity, time, and ambition.

Read on for feminine financial quotes, which will do nothing other than to inspire you. These independent women's quotes don't shy away from discussing money and its effect on power, ambition, and how it reveals the true character of others.

"Someday I want to be rich. Some people get so rich they lose all respect for humanity. That's how rich I want to be." **-Rita Rudner**

"If one is rich and one's a woman, one can be quite misunderstood."
-Katharine Graham

"If there is only one thing in my life that I am proud of, it's that I've never been a kept woman."
-Marilyn Monroe

"There are people who have money and people who are rich." **-Coco Chanel**
 "Never work just for money or for power. They won't save your soul or help you sleep at night."
-Marian Wright Edelman

"People say that money is not the key to happiness, but I always figured if you have enough money, you can have a key made." **-Joan Rivers**

"Money, if it does not bring you happiness, will at least help you be miserable in comfort."
-Helen Gurley Brown

"Fortune does not change [people], it unmasks them."
-**Suzanne Necker**

"When you're rich and famous you are the dominant force in a relationship, even if you try hard not to be. I've talked of sacrificing everything for Fleetwood Mac, but I realize now that it is simply the only thing I've ever wanted to do." -**Stevie Nicks**

"Being rich is having money; being wealthy is having time." -**Margaret Bonnano**

"Business is fun. Controlling your own destiny is fun. Creating an idea and turning it into a movie; finding an artist and guiding their career and bringing them some type of status – there's joy in that." -**Queen Latifah**

"I was lucky to have a successful career as a model, but that was just a way to pay off my student loans."
– **Padma Lakshmi**

"A woman's best protection is a little money of her own.
-**Clare Boothe Luce**

"Money is only a tool. It will take you wherever you wish, but it will not replace you as the driver." -**Ayn Rand**

"Money follows art. Money wants what it can't buy. Class and talent. And remember while there's a talent for making money, it takes real talent to know how to spend it." **-Candace Bushnell**

"I truly believe that women should be financially independent from their men. And let's face it, money gives men the power to run the show. It gives men the power to define value. They define what's sexy. And men define what's feminine. It's ridiculous." —**Beyoncé**

"By definition, saving – for anything – requires us to not get things now so we can get bigger ones later."
 -**Jean Chatzky**

"Smart women figure out what, exactly, makes them happiest. They spend generously on those things but cut out the rest." —**Laura Vanderkam**

"Save money on the big, boring stuff so you can have something left over for life's little pleasures."
 —**Elisabeth Leamy**

"Stop buying things you don't need, to impress people you don't even like." **-Suze Orman**

"I think the harder part is having the discipline to save. So my tip is: save now or pay later. Far too many people wake up in their sixties and realize they don't have enough money. I say, let go of the mentality of spending money for immediate gratification to protect yourself in the long-term." –**Jeannette Bajalia**

"It takes as much energy to wish as it does to plan."
-**Eleanor Roosevelt**

"You can tell your values by looking at our checkbook stubs." -**Gloria Steinem**

"Money is of value for what it buys, and in love, it buys time, place, intimacy, comfort and a private corner alone." -**Mae West**

"I was raised to have value for money, to have respect for money, even though you have a lot of it."
-**Jennifer Lawrence**

"You can only become truly accomplished at something you love. Don't make money your goal. Instead, pursue the things you love doing, and then do them so well that people can't take their eyes off you." -**Maya Angelou**

Spiritual Financial Quotes

Although money is essential to surviving in this world, contrary to what most people believe, you do not need a huge amount of money to live. And, *money* being "the root of all evil" has been misquoted for generations.

It is the "love of" money that makes humans fall into temptation. So, we can say that money is not bad, but just like many other of life's materials, it can be used for good or for harm.

Listed below are spiritual financial quotes. Find out what the Bible has to say about money, giving, debt, and finances as you learn to be a wise steward of the resources God has given you.

"The LORD will open the heavens, the storehouse of his bounty, to send rain on your land in season and to bless all the work of your hands. You will lend to many nations but will borrow from none."
– **Deuteronomy 28:12**

"For the love of money is the root of all evil: which while some coveted after, they have erred from the faith, and pierced themselves through with many sorrows."
-**1 Timothy 6:10**

"If a person gets his attitude toward money straight, it will help straighten out almost every other area in his life." - **Rev. Billy Graham**

"Whoever loves money never has enough; whoever loves wealth is never satisfied with their income. This too is meaningless." –**Ecclesiastes 5:10**

"Then some soldiers asked him, "And what should we do?" He replied, "Don't extort money and don't accuse people falsely—be content with your pay." – **Luke 3:14**

"Get money to live; then live and use it, else it is not true that thou hast gotten. Surely use alone makes money not contemptible." - **George Herbert**

"He that rightly understands the reasonableness and excellency of charity will know that it can never be excusable to waste any of our money in pride and folly."
- **William Law**

"If you lend money to one of my people among you who is needy, do not treat it like a business deal; charge no interest." – **Exodus 22:25**

"Let no debt remain outstanding, except the continuing debt to love one another, for whoever loves others has fulfilled the law" – **Romans 13:8**

"Better the little that the righteous have than the wealth of many wicked; 17 for the power of the wicked will be broken, but the LORD upholds the righteous."
– **Psalm 37:16-17**

"Dishonest money dwindles away, but whoever gathers money little by little makes it grow." – **Proverbs 13:11**

"Do not charge a fellow Israelite interest, whether on money or food or anything else that may earn interest."
– **Deuteronomy 23:19**

"Most people fail to realize that money is both a test and trust from God." - **Rick Warren**

"Nothing I am sure has such a tendency to quench the fire of religion as the possession of money." - **J.C. Ryle**

"Lazy hands make for poverty, but diligent hands bring wealth." - **Proverbs 10:4**

"The fellow that has no money is poor. The fellow that has nothing but money is poorer still." - **Billy Sunday**

"A man could have all the money in all the banks in all the world, and be worth nothing so far as God is concerned, if he were still living 'to and for himself!'"

- **Major Ian Thomas**

Do you spend more time thinking about money than you do thinking on the things of God? If your answer is yes you may need to take a look at your priorities. As a Christian nothing should be more important nor consume your thoughts and actions more than your relationship with the Lord. Everything you think and do should be to His glory. "Let the words of my mouth, and the meditation of my heart, be acceptable in thy sight, O Lord, my strength, and my redeemer."

-**Psalm 19:14**

ABOUT THE AUTHOR

Ebony Ormond-Ham is an accomplished Business Woman, International Speaker & Self-published Author of her book *Three Times A Lady*: **The Woman, Her Business, Her God.** Born January 29, 1982 in Kinston, N.C., to Dalton Jones and Lalonnie Rankin, Ebony was birthed into two families of entrepreneurs. The eldest of five children, and being educated in the Durham County Public School system, helped to spark a sense of self sufficiency and strength necessary to defeat the odds.

Ebony is undoubtedly your modern day Industrialist. As Chief Executive Officer of multiple multi-million dollar businesses, under the umbrella of **Eye Listen Empowerment Center, Inc**, including *Eye Listen Empowerment Center, LLC* and *Sneakerhead Youth*

Empowerment Center, she has become nationally recognized as the face of female empowerment, as she inspires women and youth to break glass ceilings through her story of poverty, faith, and wealth.

Her success story of how she purchased a multi-million-dollar company while struggling to free herself from the stigma of poverty is one that is being told globally. And, in addition to her national impact, she is an internationally sought after speaker.

Ebony has been fortunate to expand her influence as she has worked alongside some of the world's most renowned influencers; including, Dr. Juanita Bynum, Motivational Speaker Dr. Cindy Trimm, and Celebrity Wealth Management Specialist James Hunt, to name a few. Also, recognized by the *Fulton County Police Department* as the youngest African-American female to own an accredited community mental health center in Georgia, she has proven herself to be one of the most impactful female leaders of her time.

With a strong desire to empower and lead other female entrepreneurs, Ebony is now impacting and empowering women through her recently launched movement, *Three Times A Lady, Inc.* The 3TL movement is one of Atlanta's greatest self-motivating actions; inspiring leadership and enlightening aspiring women entrepreneurs of all nationalities to achieve financial stability, healthy living, professional development, and spiritual awareness.

Ebony has also launched an annually celebrated event, The **"I Conceive"** *Women's Empowerment Weekend*; which endeavors to restore hope to the 7.4+ million women who receive infertility treatment, when the path to parenthood is paved with obstacles and rough patches. For more information about Ebony Ormond-Ham, Three Times A Lady, Inc., or the Eye Listen Empowerment Center, Inc., please visit her website at www.threetimesalady.org

> *"Cast not away therefore your confidence, for it shall bring forth a great recompense of rewards."*
> ~ Hebrews 10:35